a funny little bird

a funny little bird

jennifer yerkes

sourcebooks
jabberwocky

For my two little,
funny little birds!

Once there was a funny little bird

Most of the time, it was as if he was invisible.

Or almost.

When he was seen,

other birds made fun of him.

One day he'd had enough.

He set out on his own.

On the road,

he met a magnificent bird...

...who ignored him.

The funny little bird decided not to be sad
and continued on his way,

with a souvenir under his wing,
and an idea in his head.

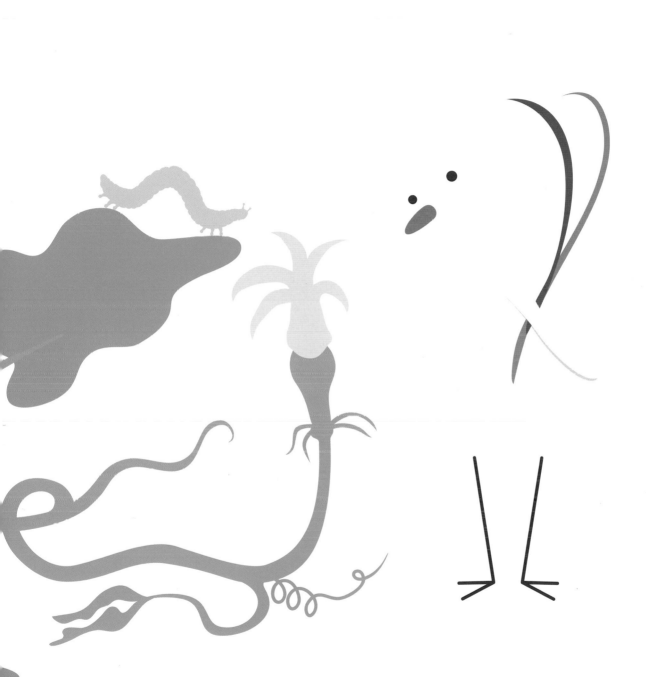

The world is full of beautiful things, he thought.

Treasures even fall from the sky!

His collection grew.

And now others started to notice him.

He became very proud.

So proud that he began to show off.

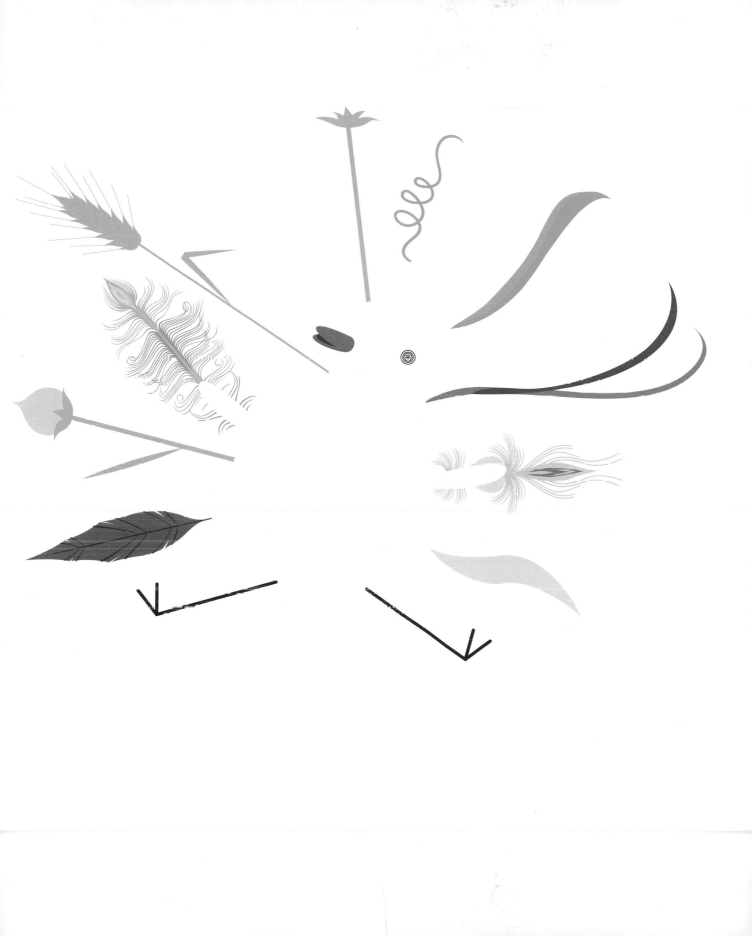

He dropped his treasures and hid.

Because if he could not be seen, he could not be caught!

The funny little bird continued on his way, his load much lighter.

Now he understood why he was special.

If danger suddenly appeared,

he could make his friends invisible too.

And together they would be safe.

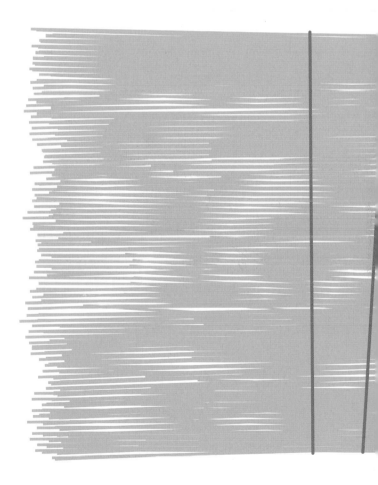

Now the funny little bird isn't alone anymore.

And he never shows off.

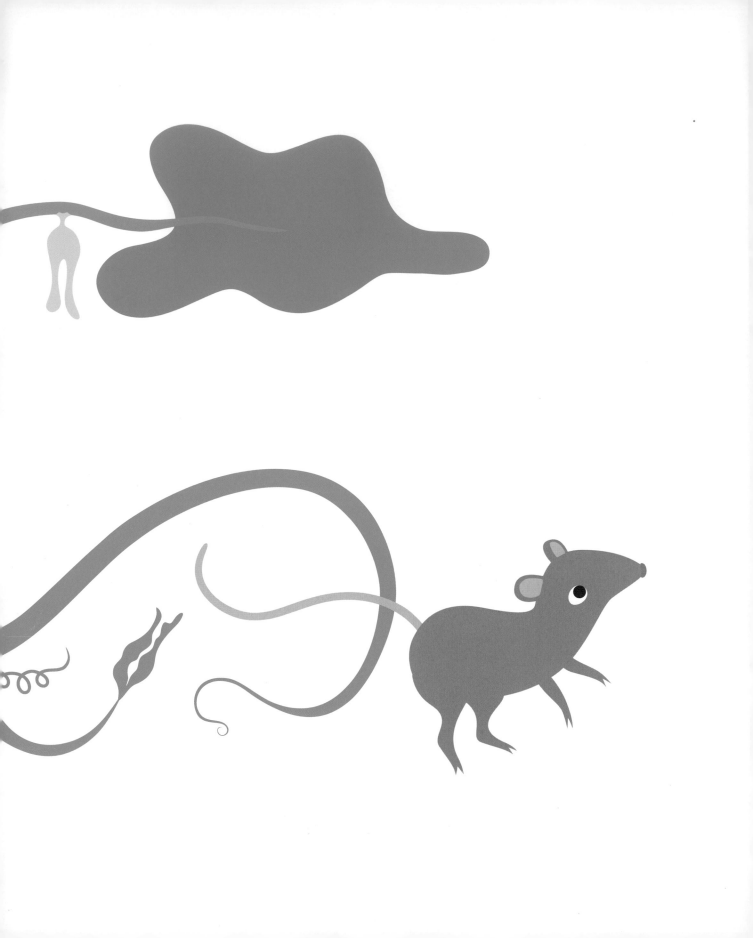

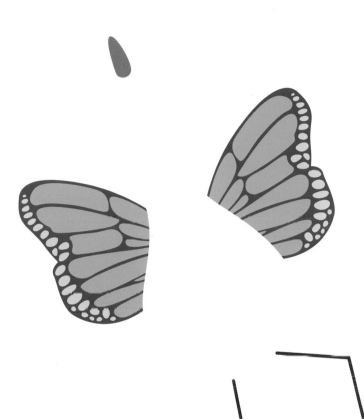

Well, almost never!